My Yer.

By Yerusalem Work

2016

Table of Contents

Part I: World Religion

The summer sun sets as two teenagers, Abdul-Tawwab and Solomon, leave a party where they met for the first time. Abdul, 17, who will soon enter his junior year in high school, walks towards his yellow sports car and Solomon, 16, follows. The car flies out of the driveway in an effort to escape an evening of debauchery. The Virginia home they exited had transformed into a lion's den. In the passenger seat, Solomon rests with his beer. Abdul quickly stops and starts at suburban intersections. He halts only for fear of being seen by police.

"Solomon, don't drink in my new car," Abdul commands. Solomon continues to sip his beer.

"I forgot Muslims don't drink alcohol. I'm glad I'm not Muslim," Solomon, a Jewish soul, responds with wanton disrespect.

Abdul-Tawwab takes his right hand off the steering wheel to remove the beer bottle from Solomon's hand.

A mother and child, Zahara and David, who are visiting a neighbor, cross the street ahead of them.

"L'chaim! You want a taste of my beer, Abdul-Tawwab?" Solomon falsely celebrates.

On this summer night, the car windows are open. Abdul grips the beer and Solomon releases the glass bottle. Then Abdul-Tawwab pours the beer out on the street through an open window.

David notices and tugs at his mother's heart strings as he asks, "Mommy, what's that?"

Zahara reassures him, "Honey, it's probably water." She doesn't want him to worry.

David astutely expresses concern, "Doesn't he know about water scarcity? Somewhere someone's thirsty."

To protect her son, Zahara reaches for David's hand as she comforts him by saying, "Let's hold hands when we cross the street."

Zahara holds her son's hand tighter as a sign of compassion. Zahara sees a neighbor with a new baby and skitters to meet her at the street corner while David remains on the road carrying a heavy backpack from a visit to the public library. David looks down and glances at his untied shoe. While in the center of the right lane, he immediately ties his shoelaces as he pauses close to the sidewalk.

In Abdul-Tawwab's car, the battle continues. Abdul argues, "It's not even legal in this country to drink at your age."

Solomon declares, "What a waste. I'm 16 and I can't have any fun."

Abdul exclaims, "You're ungrateful."

Solomon chortles, "My dad didn't buy me a new sports car with Saudi oil money. I can't be rich like you. It's a bitter disappointment."

With an air of judgment, Abdul-Tawwab exacts, "Is that why you sell drugs?"

Solomon determined, defends himself, "Drugs should be legal. If you can afford them, follow your dreams." Solomon displays a noxious smile.

Terrified, Abdul-Tawwab rends his soul. "This is a nightmare. You want a ride home. I'll take you home."

At this point, Abdul-Tawwab accelerates the sports car and they crash into David who was momentarily neglected by his mom, Zahara. She was talking to a neighbor who was pushing a stroller on the sidewalk. Abdul's car swerves onto the sidewalk, but only hits David.

Zahara sees the accident and runs toward her son. "My baby," she cries. Zahara runs to her son and holds him as his breath slows and he becomes unconscious. She screams.

Profoundly despondent, Zahara whimpers, "Help!"

The accident results in a loud thud and the neighbor calls 9-1-1. "Hurry!" the neighbor demands. She continues, "A child was struck by a car."

The 9-1-1 Dispatcher questions, "Is the child still alive?"

The neighbor calmly requests, "Please send an ambulance."

Abdul-Tawwab recovers from the impact of the air bag. The police arrive with an ambulance. Solomon ran home secretly away from the scene of the crime after barreling out of the damaged sports car. His furtive escape goes unnoticed by David's mom and the neighbor. Zahara calls out to Allah for mercy. She points her finger at Abdul-Tawwab with indignant rage. "You killed my son."

The police interrogate Abdul-Tawwab and arrest him for having an open bottle of alcohol in his car. Alarmed, Abdul gulps air. "I didn't drink it."

The police slam his head into the car as they handcuff him. The police officers use excessive force and ask no genuine questions. They read him his Miranda rights. Abdul-Tawwab cries and calls out in pain, "I can't breathe."

The police officers disregard Abdul-Tawwab's suffering. They chide, "You're going to jail."

Abdul yells, "Solomon!" with a grimace at Solomon's disappearance.

David is rushed to the hospital. He is in critical condition. Though he is in a coma, everyone searches for signs of hope. Zahara sits at his bedside with prayer beads while chanting in Arabic. She concludes with a whisper,

"Oh Allah, have mercy on us."

Inside a prison, Abdul-Tawwab sits alone in a cell with his head in his hands. He is physically distraught. Malik, Abdul-Tawwab's dad, nears the prison bars and shows the prison guard his visitor's badge.

"Your dad is here to see you," the prison guard mutters. Father and son speak through the bars for the first time since the car impelled into David, an elementary school student. Malik places his hand on his son's head while Abdul-Tawwab cries repentantly with his head down.

Malik, reticent, inquires, "Son, are you guilty of drinking and driving?"

Abdul-Tawwab firmly responds, "No, Dad. Solomon brought the beer into the car. I didn't drink it."

His father shocked retorts, "Who's Solomon?"

Abdul-Tawwab remarks, "A Jewish kid I met at a party."

Malik scolds, "Do you know him?"

Abdul-Tawwab, weakened, whines. "I met him at the party. He asked for a ride home."

Malik regaining wisdom imparts, "Where is he now?"

Abdul-Tawwab emptied of hope replies, "When I woke up after the air bag was activated, he was gone."

Malik carefully questions, "Son, I trust you. You didn't see the innocent child in front of you at the stop sign?"

"No, I didn't. Is he alive?" Abdul-Tawwab, exasperated, asks.

"He's in critical condition at a nearby hospital. Let's pray he lives through this," urges Malik.

Abdul-Tawwab beleaguered chimes in, "What about Solomon?"

Malik resounds, "He's not your friend. Forgive and forget."

Abdul-Tawwab regaining clarity offers proof of his innocence, "Dad, ask the police to give me a Breathalyzer test so they realize I wasn't drinking."

Malik heartened responds, "OK, son. We'll get through this."

The father and son exchange tearful, worried glances and the prison guard escorts Malik out. At the door, Malik has an inaudible, private conversation with the police. Moments later the same police officer who arrested Abdul-Tawwab approaches his cell.

The police officer speaks with a tone of authority, "Your father asked us to give you a Breathalyzer. He says you weren't drinking."

Abdul-Tawwab insists, "No, officer, I wasn't drinking. I gave someone a ride home and he's the one who brought the alcohol into the car. I'll never do that again."

The police officer reminds Abdul-Tawwab, "Looks like someone got you in a lot of trouble."

After a brief alcohol test, Abdul-Tawwab walks in a straight line. The police officer announces, "Zero blood alcohol content. It looks like you were not drinking. Who was the mysterious man with you in your car? The police saw you alone."

Abdul-Tawwab commits himself to the truth, "I only know his first name – Solomon."

Intrigued the police officer relishes in determining guilt, "Was he drinking under age?"

"Yes," Abdul-Tawwab reports.

The police officer returns with the statement, "No one else saw him at the scene of the crime." He offers passing advice, "It looks like you shouldn't drive with tinted windows."

Abdul-Tawwab unmoved, "It's a sports car."

The police officer admonishes, "Do you have 'a need for speed'?"

Abdul-Tawwab sarcastically remarks, "My thoughts run lightning fast."

The police officer picks up the pace, "How many fingers am I holding up?" The officer clasps his hands and holds a fist up.

"Zero," Abdul-Tawwab tolerates.

The police officer acknowledges, "Muslims gave us the concept of zero."

Abdul-Tawwab wryly spits out, "I've never seen someone so thankful for nothing."

The police officer offers hope and a stern warning, "If that little boy you crashed into survives this accident, there's a good chance the parents will drop the charges. Otherwise, you'll be in prison the rest of your teenage existence and well into adulthood."

Words rise out of Abdul-Tawwab in a moment of despair, "This nightmare has to end."

The police officer establishes the importance of faith, "Pray for the well-being of that precious child you crashed into. He may live to forgive you."

Alert, Abdul-Tawwab asks, "What's his name?"

The police officer provides a message that resonates with Abdul-Tawwab, an imprisoned soul, "David. His father was on the nightly news with the announcement that if his son, David, lives through this, he'll ask for all the charges to be dropped. David's father, Ibrahim, heard you were a good student and that you normally stay out of trouble. A news reporter interviewed your dad, who also defended you. The community wants what's best for both you and David. All is not lost."

Abdul-Tawwab, resolute, states, "I'll pray."

The police officer leaves him in a barely lit prison cell through the watches of the night. After midnight, Abdul-Tawwab prays *tahajjud*. His incessant *dua* is his only consolation. At one point, his teardrops reach the floor and at the same moment, it is *fajr*.

Zahara's head is to the floor in prayer. She lifts her face, while in a kneeling position and whispers *"As-salaamu alaikum wa rahmatullah"* to her right and left wiping the tears from her eyes. She recites Islamic blessings on her prayer beads. The hospital door opens. Her son is being wheeled in. He is then situated in his bed in the center of the room.

Zahara holds his right hand. Before the nurse exits and closes the door, the kind nurse looks compassionately at Zahara.

The nurse confidently intimates, "We have hope David will wake up any minute."

Zahara begs for understanding as she begins to collapse on David's hospital bed, "I love my child. I wish I had not let go of his hand as we crossed the street. It's my fault."

Before another tear can drop, David wakes up. His eyes flutter.

David awakens and inspires, "Mom, Allah is Most Merciful, Most Compassionate."

Zahara utters in a state of shock and subtle disbelief, "Can you hear my voice? I love you, David. Forgive Mommy." She is worried these may be her last words to her son.

David assures her, "I forgive you, Mommy."

David lifts his head a little in the intensive care unit. The nurse returns having heard their conversation.

"*Mashallah*, I'm alive to see the return of mother and child. David, don't move too much. Let's wait 'til you're more stable. I'll call the doctors. We have good news to report," proudly exclaims the nurse.

"*Subhanallah*, I'll tell Ibrahim," Zahara matches the nurse's joy.

Zahara exits the hospital room and the nurse calls the doctors with the red hospital phone. Ibrahim, Zahara's husband, receives a phone call on his cell. Zahara had charged her phone through the sleepless night. Ibrahim is home getting ready to work at the office. Zahara shares the good news.

"Ibrahim, David is speaking. He's out of the coma." She is proud to be the bearer of good news.

"*Subhanallah*, our son is conscious," he exclaims with exquisite joy, "When can we bring him home?"

Zahara, upbeat, expectantly replies, "I'll ask the doctors. Will you be here soon?"

"Yes, I'm on my way." He grabs his car keys and walks to the garage, "Work can wait. They'll understand. Zahara…" He turns the engine on. It is a bright summer morning.

"Yes, honey," she appreciates his loving tone.

Ibrahim suggests, "Let's not press charges against the driver. Let's release Abdul-Tawwab from prison. He's a first offender. We don't need to see him live his life behind bars. David is alive. He will be well *In Shaa Allah*. Let's not waste precious youth."

Zahara adamantly states, "Abdul-Tawwab can't go unpunished."

Ibrahim exhorts, "We can recommend community service, but he has enough weight on his shoulders. His mother passed away last year. Malik, Abdul-Tawwab's father, told me. Maybe that's why Abdul engaged in this reckless behavior."

Zahara winces.

"Oh, I understand." She continues, "Forgiven. If David can forgive me, I can forgive Abdul-Tawwab."

Ibrahim expresses wholeheartedly, "Please forgive yourself. You walked away from David for a moment."

Zahara realizes, "We were separated for moments and look what happened."

Knowingly, Ibrahim recommends, "Imagine. Abdul-Tawwab was separated from his mom for a year and this is what happened to him. Let's pray."

He drives closer and closer to the hospital, cautious of his speed. He parks in the hospital garage.

Zahara resigns, "Pray for a blessing." She is torn between her phone call with Ibrahim and her responsibility to eye David's hospital room. Her straight, black Persian hair, the color of oil or her dilated pupil, carries depth, volume and grace. Her hair touches her shoulders. Her diamond necklace glitters in the incandescent hospital lights. She exudes the heights of culture and class.

They drop their phones – him in his leather briefcase, her in her purse. Ibrahim scurries to the intensive care unit without flowers or balloons, with only his heartfelt hope. He faces his wife, Zahara, of over a decade and hugs her as he uplifts with the message, "You are a blessing."

Zahara embraces him with the words, "I love you, Ibbi."

Ibrahim confidently affirms, "I love you more, Zahara. More and more each day."

In the afternoon at the height of the summer sun, the police officer opens Abdul-Tawwab's prison door.

The police officer proclaims, "You're a free man, Abdul-Tawwab. David is alive and well. He forgives you. David's family requires you perform community service until you graduate from high school."

Abdul-Tawwab, blessed, questions the officer. "Am I free to go home?"

"Yes, your dad, Malik, is here."

Abdul-Tawwab walks out of the prison cell and his belongings are returned to him. The police officer, Malik and Abdul-Tawwab stand remorsefully, yet joyfully looking at each other.

Abdul-Tawwab emerges triumphant, "Dad, I agree to do community service."

Malik relieved says to him, "I'm glad you're safe."

Abdul-Tawwab, feeling discouraged, says, "I wish mom were here."

Malik with a contorted smile and a hushed voice advises, "We can visit her grave."

Abdul-Tawwab affirms, "Let's go soon."

Eighth grade middle school children play soccer in a park next to a cemetery. The autumn leaves fall. The field is covered in a blanket of crisp, multi-colored leaves - red, yellow, and brown. A "straight path" is clear for Mohammed, who scores a goal. Ahmed, the goalkeeper, tosses the ball to a teammate to continue the game.

Malik drives Abdul-Tawwab to visit his mother's grave at the Muslim cemetery next to the soccer park. They stand facing the tombstone that says her name "Noor, dearly beloved..."

Abdul-Tawwab utters under his breath, "I wish I could be with you."

Malik interjects, "Son, don't say that. Be thankful you're alive."

"Mom, I miss you so much," Abdul-Tawwab admits the pain and loss in his life.

Abdul-Tawwab cries and his father holds him.

Malik lectures, "Trust in Allah, son. Do good deeds. Study the Qur'an. For believers, there is no fear and no grief."

Abdul-Tawwab recognizes an opportunity, "There are so many leaves covering the park and the cemetery. It serves as a metaphor. It's like we're buried beneath a blanket of sin."

"We all sin," Malik presides, "but the Prophet Mohammad, *SalAllahu Alaihi Wa Salam*, said that your sins will fall away like leaves from a tree when you offer your *Salat* to please Allah."

"Dad, may I remove the leaves from the ground as my community service project?"

Malik happily encourages, "I think it's a good idea. I'll share your idea with others to see if we can get the green light. We all want to be cleansed of sin."

Abdul-Tawwab maturely states his wish, "I want to be far removed from sin."

"Keep making *Salat*," his father emboldens him.

"Do you think David really forgave me?" Abdul asks quizzically.

"He and his family forgave you. Trust me," Malik openly states.

Abdul-Tawwab then ponders, "Can I trust myself?"

Malik confides, "You will be tested, but you can trust yourself."

Malik and Abdul-Tawwab walk away from the grave. Malik's arm is around Abdul-Tawwab's shoulders.

In the middle school hallway on the following day, the children from the soccer game are at their lockers.

Fatima, a headstrong pre-teen, investigates, "Ahmed, who won yesterday's game?"

Ahmed repeats for the tenth time that day, "Mohammed's team."

Mohammed modestly deflects attention, "Who's keeping score?"

Ahmed playfully irate responds, "You're the only one who scored a goal, modest Mohammed."

Mohammed, Ahmed and Fatima walk in the religious studies classroom and everyone is seated. The sign at the front of the classroom indicates the subject is "World Religion." Dr. Aisha, the teacher, prepares the class for an exam.

Dr. Aisha waits for the bell to ring and then initiates the first question, "Do Muslims believe in Original Sin?"

Fatima boldly raises her hand.

Dr. Aisha orders, "Fatima, please respond."

Fatima bravely states, "No, Dr. Aisha. Islam reveals Prophet Adam, peace be upon him, was taught words of repentance. Original Sin is a Christian concept not accepted in Islam or Judaism."

Fatima straightens her glasses, which were falling down her nose.

"Excellent response," Dr. Aisha excitedly reinforces. "There is forgiveness in Islam. Remember the importance of sincere repentance. Our exam will be one week from today."

The day following the exam, the students return to the park. It is after school on a fall day. The wind moves unpredictably. Abdul-Tawwab, a high school student and a park attendant, collects all of the fallen leaves before the middle schoolers play soccer.

Ahmed, surprised, says, "Abdul-Tawwab, you drive a yellow sports car and you're doing community service. *Mashallah!*"

Abdul-Tawwab esteemed highly speaks with dignity, "Not anymore. I don't need a sports car. I prefer something sensible. I sped through an intersection. This is my community service project. I volunteered to clear the playing field."

Ahmed clumsily follows, "I remember you put David in the hospital."

Abdul-Tawwab reluctantly responds, "Thanks for reminding me."

Ahmed reassures him, "But he's alive today. It's a miracle." Ahmed bounces the soccer ball on his thighs, alternating legs.

Mohammed leads with a question, "Will you be our referee?"

Abdul-Tawwab, like a father, assures, "Yes, I'll keep certain you play fair."

The boys begin to play soccer with more freedom of movement. The next day at school in the classroom, the blackboard is empty. Before class begins, the students are seated.

"Good game yesterday?" Fatima fearlessly broaches the subject of soccer.

Ahmed, this time confident, proclaims, "3-3 tie."

Mohammed explains, "No leaves to contend with. More freedom to pursue our goals." He performs a signature handshake with Ahmed.

"It was a fair competition," Ahmed clarifies. "Brother Abdul-Tawwab swept away all of the leaves on the soccer field. His community service allowed us to actually run full speed."

"What required Abdul to do community service?" Fatima asks unsure.

Ahmed reminds her, "Remember David was hit by a car. It was Abdul-Tawwab's car."

Mohammed contributes to the conversation, "Why does a teenager need a sports car?"

Ahmed clearly estimates, "Ego."

Fatima abashedly includes, "Abdul-Tawwab's mom passed away last year. His father probably bought him a new shiny car to help him forget."

Dr. Aisha overhears the students' conversation as she walks in the classroom door with the graded exam papers in her hand.

Dr. Aisha engages in the discussion with her star pupils, "You never forget the loss of a loved one, but you can heal."

Fatima expresses great concern, "David almost lost his life."

Dr. Aisha rids them all of worry, "God is gracious and merciful. He preserved David's life. David can teach us all a lesson in forgiveness. Abdul could be in a lot of trouble right now for reckless driving."

Mohammed needs the message of forgiveness underscored. "But David's family forgave him?"

Dr. Aisha expertly remarks, "Yes, Mohammed, it's important to practice forgiveness. We should not be remembered for our sins, but the good we do. Speaking of the good, many of you received good scores on your exam. One person scored perfect."

Fatima with an air of absurdity, "Let me guess."

The entire class shouts, "Mohammed!"

Dr. Aisha does not see the need to expound on the subject, "Correct."

Mohammed humbly replies, "All praise to Allah."

Dr. Aisha passes out the test results and invites the students to ask informal questions. "You can ask any question you want related to world religion."

The teacher, a doctor of education, walks through the aisles and distributes the individual papers onto the students' desks.

Ahmed begins, "If life's a game, how do we learn the rules?"

Dr. Aisha jumps at the chance to answer this question, "We follow the *Sunnah* of the Prophet Muhammad, *SalAllahu alayhi wasalam...*"

Ahmed debates, "But life has changed so much since the Qur'an was first revealed."

Dr. Aisha appreciates his philosophy, but rebuts, "Our class today will prove to us that the most important questions in life have not changed and neither have the answers. Let's focus."

Dr. Aisha steps up to the blackboard and writes the word "*Jahiliyyah*." She circles it.

She continues, "The world is no longer in the age of ignorance that preceded the revelation of the Qur'an. We have moved out of the darkness and into the..."

In unison, the class yells, "Light!"

Dr. Aisha nods her head in agreement while facing the class. She raises her chin - proud of the students - turns around and continues to write on the chalkboard.

In the following week, Abdul-Tawwab clears leaves from the cemetery. He sees David walk on crutches with flowers toward Noor's grave. Ibrahim and Zahara stand by their black and silver SUV. They watch David place the flowers on Noor's grave. David meets Abdul-Tawwab face-to-face.

David sorrowfully sends his greeting, *"As-salamu alaikum*, Abdul-Tawwab. I'm sorry you lost your mom."

Abdul-Tawwab greets him, *"Wa-alaikum as-salaam.* David, you remember me?"

David smiles after having done his research. "I know a little bit about you. We come from a close-knit community."

Abdul-Tawwab speaks with mixed emotion of fear and hope, "I don't like who I am in your story. Please forgive me. It's a miracle you're walking."

David wisely assures, "Allah is known for miracles. Life is filled with miracles."

Abdul-Tawwab, his heart catching up with his head, expresses his gratitude, "You brought flowers to my mother's grave? May Allah bless you."

David speaks knowingly, "It's not easy to be separated from your mother. At her feet are the gates to Paradise."

Abdul-Tawwab honors him, "You're a wise child."

"The Qur'an and Hadith give us pearls of wisdom." David enjoys referring to the sources of his faith. "I forgive you."

Ibrahim and Zahara witness the conversation. Then they approach Abdul-Tawwab and David.

Zahara issues forth her first words to Abdul since the car crash, "We forgive you."

Ibrahim places his hand on Abdul-Tawwab's shoulder and faces him like a father.

Ibrahim consoles, "Now you know Allah's love extends beyond the grave. Your mother would want to see you happy and successful. Think of us as extended family."

Abdul-Tawwab drops the rake and they all hug in a circle with Ibrahim and David next to Abdul-Tawwab on opposite sides and Zahara across from Abdul.

Zahara, effusive, pours out from her heart, "We love you. Though we can't fill the space in your heart reserved for your mother, we can show you the loving-kindness you deserve as her son."

Abdul-Tawwab demonstrates his faith with a blessing. "May Allah bless you a thousandfold."

The wind blows the leaves away from his mother's plaque on her grave. The engraved words are "Noor, dearly beloved and close to Allah *Subhanahu Wa Ta'ala*,

her Beloved."

Part II: A Mother's Love

Noor and Malik drink tea in their living room. Abdul-Tawwab, a sophomore in high school, walks home from soccer practice. He opens the door and takes off his shoes. He is only 16.

The Qur'an is playing as Malik smiles to say, "Welcome home, son."

"Dad, we won." Abdul-Tawwab breathes heavily from overexertion. "Our team's won every game this season." Abdul drops the soccer ball and kisses his parents' cheeks.

Malik proudly encourages his son and pats him on the back, "The reigning champions…"

Abdul-Tawwab slows down, "So far…we have a soccer tournament next week. Mom, Dad – can you make it?"

Noor introduces a grave topic, "I have chemotherapy. I'll be in the hospital. If only I can win my battle with cancer…"

Abdul-Tawwab expresses his wish, "You will, Mom. I'm only in high school. I need you here with me."

Noor barely has the energy to hug her son. As she rises, they embrace and he sits next to her. "Abdul-Tawwab, there's nothing I want more than to see you through college. Make *dua* for me. Aunt Saha visited this afternoon. Hopefully, you'll see her next time. She brought you dessert."

Abdul-Tawwab beams, "My favorite one from Afghanistan?"

Malik joins in the amazement, "Yes, honey. Sweet, sticky rice. Noor, let's ask Aunt Saha to come for dinner next week. Abdul, please set the table."

Abdul-Tawwab stands to his feet and walks to the dining room where the dessert is at the center of the table.

Noor pries, "Malik, do we have enough water? You must be thirsty after the game, Abdul sweetheart."

"Yes, Mom, I am. What's for dinner?" He innocently asks.

Malik pours three glasses of water. Abdul sets the dining room table.

"We have enough water for a camel to drink," Malik jocularly whims.

Abdul-Tawwab always fond of his father's humor responds, "*Alhamdulillah.*"

Abdul begins to drink from his glass of water. Noor turns off the TV. The phone rings. Noor sees the caller ID. It is her doctor. She extends a greeting, "*As-salamu alaikum.*"

Dr. Ali responds appropriately, "*Wa-alaikum as-salam.* Is this Noor?"

"Yes."

Dr. Ali proceeds with confidential information, "The reports don't look good. We need to admit you to the hospital. Please check-in tonight."

"Yes, Dr. Ali. After dinner…" Noor agrees.

She hangs up the phone with a heavy heart. She joins her husband and son for dinner.

Noor shares the bad news, "Dr. Ali needs me to check-in the hospital tonight."

Malik holds her hand and asks for her patience, "After dinner, honey."

Abdul-Tawwab offers humor, "Life's short, Mom. Eat the dessert first."

They sit at the table holding hands. The water and dessert are on the table.

Noor appreciates the humor, but with a quiet tone prays aloud, "Oh Allah, have mercy on us."

Noor whose hair is white and sparse, kisses her son's full head of hair as he bows to her. They eat two bites.

Noor, pretending to be full, excuses herself from the table and rushes around the house. "Let me put on my *hijab*."

Malik lets go of his fork and leaves the table, "I'll get the car."

Malik exits to the garage where their mini-van is parked. Noor places a blue and purple vibrantly colored *hijab* on her head. She picks up her purse. The grumble from the car Malik started is both heard and felt.

Abdul-Tawwab stands at the door, "You look beautiful, Mom."

"Thank you, honey." She smiles with her eyes and wants to comfort him.

Abdul-Tawwab regales her, "Our camel awaits."

Noor steps outside, "I hope this is a short visit."

Abdul-Tawwab extends hope, "We'll be home soon."

Abdul-Tawwab and Noor join Malik in the van. The phone rings in their living room. It's Aunt Saha. The voice recording plays as they drive to the hospital.

Aunt Saha speaks endearingly with an Afghan accent, "*As-salamu alaikum*, sweethearts. How was dessert? Did Abdul-Tawwab enjoy it?"

Later that night in the hospital, Noor sits up in bed. Malik and Abdul-Tawwab are still with her. Noor is reading the Qur'an in its English translation.

Noor recites half to the room and half to herself, "Certainly, the help of Allah is near" (Quran 2:214).

Abdul-Tawwab sweetly boasts, "My mother, the Islamic Scholar."

Malik paces as he repeats again and again, "The doctor should return with good news."

Noor puts her trust in Allah. "I'm in critical condition, honey. Allah knows best."

Malik faces his wife and son with a look of fatigue and determination. "I checked our voicemail. Sister Saha says, '*As-salamu alaikum.*'"

Noor is beside herself with pleasure, "Please ask her to visit."

Abdul-Tawwab with his good manners requests his father, "Dad, tell her thank you for dessert."

Noor adds, "And thank you for the *hijab*. She was with me in my darkest hour."

Malik, with an air of hope, grumbles, "This is not the end."

The hospital machines make noise and soon there is a flat line. Then Noor's heart activity delicately returns.

"Mom, no…" Abdul-Tawwab wishes he could restore his mother to good health.

Abdul-Tawwab cries and holds her hand.

Malik offers help, "I'll call the doctor." Next, he exits the hospital room.

Malik rushes into the hospital hallway and tells the world, "My wife needs a doctor. She's reached her last breath."

The nurses swarm into Noor's room and the doctor is called on the intercom.

Safe from the commotion, as if in the eye of a tornado, Abdul-Tawwab gazes at his mom in perfect stillness knowing this could be the last time. He gently says, "Mom, I love you."

Noor does not hesitate. "I love you too, honey."

Malik returns to Noor's bedside.

Malik with great care urges, "Don't give up."

"Be strong for Abdul-Tawwab," she murmurs. "I love you both sincerely."

Malik in desperate calm breathes in, "My beloved…"

Noor exhales, "Habibi."

Dr. Ali rushes into the hospital room. He hurriedly states, "Noor, we need to run more tests."

The machine flat lines with finality.

Dr. Ali scrounges up courage, "I need the nurses here with me. Can we bring Noor back to life?"

Nurse Naala guides Malik and Abdul-Tawwab outside of the hospital room.

"Thank you for your patience," Naala consoles in a professional demeanor. "Please allow us to operate on Noor. The cancer has spread."

Malik tearfully begs, "Will I ever see my wife again?"

Naala muses, "If not now, then in *Jannah, In Shaa Allah*. Please standby. We'll update you throughout the night."

Malik calls Aunt Saha. "*Salam alaikum*, Sister Saha, Noor is in critical condition. She may not live through the evening."

Aunt Saha stunned replies, "She's fought breast cancer this long. I hope she'll make it through tonight."

"If not, know that you are dear to us. Noor thanked you for the *hijab* and Abdul-Tawwab for dessert. You're his favorite aunt," Malik assured.

Aunt Saha inspires confidence, "We'll always be like family."

"*Subhanallah*, we love you."

"I love you, Aunt Saha," Abdul-Tawwab calls out.

The night in the hospital becomes morning and Sheikh Shakir visits.

Sheikh Shakir greets Malik with his voice coiled, "*As-salamu alaikum warahmatulahi wa barakatuh*, I heard the news that Noor is here in the hospital. Is she still alive?"

Malik replies, "*Wa-alaikum as-salaam.* Dr. Ali is still working with her to see if he can revive her. We heard her flat line last night."

Dr. Ali walks into the hallway.

Dr. Ali dejected states, "There's nothing more we can do. Your wife was pronounced dead at 4:00 a.m. this morning."

Sheikh Shakir is the first to say, "*Inna Lillahi wa inna ilaihi raji'un.*"

Abdul-Tawwab naturally depends on the adults for answers, "I love my Mom. Why did she die?"

Dr. Ali does not answer directly, but offers consolation, "Your mom was brave. She struggled. She's not suffering now."

Malik wraps his arm around his son's shoulder. "We'll always have sweet memories. Sheikh Shakir, will you help us with the burial?"

"Yes, we'll take you through the proper steps for the *Janazah*. May Allah bless you and guide you. Noor loved you both and her light shined in the community. She was dear to so many people..." Sheikh Shakir was always a comforting voice.

Dr. Ali echoes, "She was pure sunshine. And now her body can rest."

Later that afternoon, Malik and Abdul-Tawwab drive home in the van.

Recognizing the depths of the loss, Abdul-Tawwab sadly ejects, "Dad, I miss mom."

"Me, too, son."

"We're driving so slowly," Abdul-Tawwab's mind racing.

"We don't want to get in an accident. We should be extra careful and take care of each other the way your mother wanted," Malik admonishes.

"Dad, I'll help in any way I can," Abdul rises to the occasion.

Malik, as he mourns, assuages, "I love you, son. Sorry we lost your mother."

"It's not your fault," Abdul-Tawwab hopes to ameliorate the situation.

Malik strives to take responsibility and share the burden, "I'll call Aunt Saha when we get home and ask her to help with the *Janazah* arrangements."

"Do you think Mom feels any pain?" Abdul-Tawwab questions.

"Not anymore. She is blessed. She is with her Beloved, Allah." Malik concludes as they park in the garage where there is a weight and emptiness from Noor's tragic loss.

Part III: Aylan

In a northern Virginia suburban high school, Yerusalem, 16, and Jennifer, her elder by a year, visit their lockers at the end of the day in the middle of the week. They stuff their backpacks with books and stand in the hallway. Their parents are already on their way to pick them up.

Jennifer asks for the umpteenth time, "Why do you want to convert to Islam?"

Yerusalem dances around the issue, "I want to pray in Arabic."

Jennifer, melodramatic and irate, issues forth with passion, "You can be Christian and pray in any language. As long as your prayers come from the heart, you can reach God."

"It's true. God knows the heart," Yerusalem accedes. Then she makes the conversation more personal. "However, I want to recite the Qur'an. It brings me peace."

Jennifer, sounding disturbed, complains, "What about *wudu*, the ritual ablutions preceding prayer? That would cause me anxiety."

Yerusalem extols, "It's a way to cleanse or purify the body and soul. We sin in different ways. *Wudu* prepares us for repentance and shields us from future sin. To face the King, Al-Malik, in prayer requires sanctity, dignity and respect."

Abdul-Tawwab, 18, a senior in high school, glides through the hallway to pick up his books and to walk to the parking lot. He enters the conversation with a snide remark.

"My dad is named Malik, but he's not the One you're praying to."

Yerusalem quickly transforms the conversation into a theological discussion. "Allah *subhanahu wa ta'ala* is not anyone's father."

"God is my father," Jennifer protests recalcitrant.

"If Adam was born without a mother or a father, why do Christians cling to being children of God when most often they know who their biological parents are?" Yerusalem asks with half-hearted curiosity.

Jennifer retorts, "Because Jesus is the Son of God, I am no longer a servant. I am a child of God. I was baptized and you were too, Yerusalem. You're still Christian in my book."

Abdul-Tawwab, who admires Yerusalem, interjects, "I thought you reverted to Islam."

They exit the hallway and walk onto the pavement.

"Yes, I did, Abdul," she replies as if being interviewed on-camera. "*As-salamu alaikum*, brother.

Jennifer, I wish you would accept me as Muslim. I'm still your friend."

The students carry heavy backpacks and take out an afternoon snack. Jennifer bites into an apple.

"I'm sorry, but I can't accept this change," Jennifer derides. "I see you as my ballerina friend."

Yerusalem, offended, becomes analytical, "Ballet is good exercise, but dance is a language and sometimes I prefer a profound silence."

Commence hearing the sound of cars driving by, doors opening and closing.

Yerusalem wishes she could be esoteric. She proclaims, once more as if on-camera, "I study the prophets. *Isa Alaihi Salaam* said, 'Blessed are the peacemakers, for they will be called the children of God.'"

Jennifer flattered responds, "I thought you didn't believe God produced children."

Abdul-Tawwab quickly grasps, "I think Yeru wants to be a peacemaker."

Jennifer waves at her mom and walks toward her car, however reluctantly, not wanting the conversation to end.

"You're like a sister to me, Yerusalem," Jennifer tries to bridge the racial divide and cross color lines. Jennifer's skin is as pale as moonlight and Yerusalem is more ebony than ivory.

"We are brothers and sisters in the human family and I know we used to be sisters in Christ. Now I'm a sister, a Muslimah. You can be too. Join the ummah, the Muslim community," as if giving an impromptu speech.

Jennifer recollects, "We used to read the Bible together."

"Let's read the Qur'an together in English. You'll find it most inspiring."

Jennifer shrugs, "I can't. I'm Christian."

Yerusalem cautions her, "Atifri. Do not fear."

Jennifer's brown eyes gleam, "A phrase I remember from our Amharic sessions. Atifri, Yerusalem, ehiteh, my sister. The sisterhood is strong, *hijab* or no *hijab*. I don't want to lose you to your Muslimah friends."

A group of Muslimahs in multi-colored, designer *hijab* walk toward their respective parents' vehicles. They simultaneously wave at Yerusalem and nod exchanging greetings.

"That's my greatest struggle these days. Should I cover?" Yerusalem confesses.

Abdul-Tawwab solves the equation, "You wear *hijab* to pray?"

"Yes, I do."

Abdul-Tawwab, in unintended rhyme, "What stops you from wearing *hijab* the rest of the day?"

"My mother won't let me," Yerusalem says with a pout.

In solidarity, Jennifer relates, "My mom wouldn't let me either. She's too liberal to realize she's conservative. And here she is. I'll see you tomorrow, sis."

Yerusalem, like a movie star, says farewell, "Ciao, darling."

Abdul and Yerusalem stand beside each other. Yerusalem nervously drops her journal onto the ground. Abdul-Tawwab picks it up, like a gentleman. It opens to the first page and underlined in huge bold letters is the word "JINN!"

Abdul-Tawwab perplexed delves into the subject, "Sister, sorry I saw your notebook. Do you see jinn?"

"You probably think I'm crazy, but yes. I have seen jinn."

"When, sister? I need the whole story," insists Abdul delaying his drive home.

Yerusalem exhales and shudders, "I prayed *Maghrib* in my bedroom, quietly so my parents would not hear me. The door to my bathroom was open. I saw a jinn, a creature of smokeless fire, carrying a cross up a hill. Immediately, I thought it was Judas. The name Judas came to mind as if I had ekphrasis."

Appreciating Yerusalem's wealth of knowledge, Abdul-Tawwab asks, "What's ekphrasis?"

She professes, "It's a Greek word meaning the power to describe a scene from a work-of-art or to translate an image into commentary. This time, I realize, it was Judas on the cross."

To see if her knowledge coincides with an authoritative Islamic source, he shares, "In the Qur'an, it says someone with the likeness of *Isa Alaihi Salaam* died

on the cross. Are you sure it was Judas?"

"I can only tell you what I saw," she clears up.

"It's as if God wants you to know the truth," Abdul

says in awe.

Yerusalem winnows, "You're the first person I told.

I'm afraid to tell anyone else."

Abdul-Tawwab reflects, "Why don't you do

ruqiya?"

Yerusalem adamantly declares, "I won't ask anyone

to perform *ruqiya* for me. I do *ruqiya* on my own. It

assures the possibility of avoiding Judgment Day. I would

love a direct ticket to Paradise."

Abdul-Tawwab honors her logic, "So would all of

us…"

Yerusalem wrests her heart from his hand and

attempts to humor him, "My mother is here. At her feet are

the gates to Paradise. I'm glad her foot is on the brake. When she dropped me off this morning, the car did not fully stop. She is always on her phone unaware of her surroundings. I'm lucky to be alive."

With a serious tone and a breathtaking smile, he shoulders the responsibility of teaching her to thank Allah, "You're blessed to still have your mother with you."

"Yes, I am. Your mother, Noor, of blessed memory remained beautiful throughout her battle with cancer. She radiated wisdom," delighted to end on a warm note.

"Thank you!" He then warns, "She did not wear *hijab* until the later stages of the disease. You have a choice. Remember."

Boldly defiant, Yerusalem, puts her scarf on as *hijab* and runs to her mother's car. "Let's see if my mom will notice. Ciao Abdul."

As she opens the door to her mother's vehicle, Yerusalem turns to Abdul-Tawwab for one more glance.

"You look beautiful," he respectfully describes Yerusalem. He remembers the last woman he told she was beautiful was his mother. He places his hand on his heart.

Yerusalem and Rachel, her mom, sit in their car, aimless.

Rachel stunned asks, "Yerusalem, what is that on your head?"

Yerusalem dutifully responds, "It's a *hijab*. It's distinctive, like a kippah." Yerusalem tries to appeal to Rachel's Jewish sensibilities.

Rachel, argumentative, dissuades, "Why are you trying to impress a boy?"

Yerusalem astounded argues her position, "I'm not trying to impress anyone. I have the freedom to wear *hijab*. I wish you would allow me to wear *hijab* before I'm your age. Abdul's mom, Noor, only wore *hijab* after she was diagnosed with cancer."

Rachel reticent, "For some, it takes a calamity. OK, if you want to wear *hijab*, honey, I accept your freedom to choose."

Yerusalem, amazed, "Really, mom?! I can wear *hijab*."

"Yes, honey. Noor was a darling. I miss her precious smile," Rachel gathers her thoughts.

Yerusalem caringly responds, "Abdul misses her more than words can say. Mom, can we go *hijab* shopping?"

"Of course, sweetie. You'll be the belle of the ball," Rachel overstates.

Yerusalem distances herself from the beauty war, "Mother, everyone is beautiful. We are only elevated based on piety."

Rachel moves the car abruptly in the direction of the mall. She proudly boasts, "My daughter, the Islamic scholar."

"My mother, the impatient one. Let's be among *As-Sabrin*, the patient ones," Yerusalem musters up Qur'anic vocabulary.

Rachel, inquisitive, asks, "Is that an Arabic word?"

"Yes, mommy, *as-sabrin* means 'the patient ones'. It's in the Qur'an."

Rachel impressed, "We'll sign you up for Arabic lessons. Since you take ballet less often, this is the perfect time to pursue a new language."

Yerusalem is thrilled. "Wow, mom! Your heart just opened up."

"I want you to look back on your life with contentment. If you choose the Straight Path, I'll be right behind you." Rachel is tempted to honk at the car in front of her for not moving fast enough when the light turns green.

"Mom, are you converting to Islam?" Yerusalem begins excitedly, as if a prayer had been answered.

Rachel calms down, "Yerusalem is Muslim. Rachel is the Mother of a Believer."

"I love you, Mom," Yerusalem is comforted enough to ask a religious studies question, "Do you think the prophets were Jewish or Muslim?"

"I love you, too, honey," Rachel responds without pausing. "Didn't you say we're all born Muslim and then some of us become Christian or Jewish?"

"Yes, I was quoting someone," Yerusalem carries the conversation, "We convert to Christianity or Judaism if we desire, but our souls are naturally good and we are born monotheists."

Rachel chooses a question she'd be too shy to ask a religious scholar, "If that's true, what religion was Abraham?"

"He was Muslim."

"I thought Abraham was Jewish," Rachel said disconcerted.

"The term Judaism comes from the tribe of Judah. Judah was a descendant of Abraham. Abraham was not Jewish," Yerusalem argues using the pure logic of a teenage novice.

"So either way, it's revisionist history," Rachel comments.

Yerusalem launches into *da'wah*, "The Prophet Muhammad, peace and blessings be upon him, was born in the 6th century of the Common Era. However, Islam is simply submission to the will of Allah, which occurred before the Common Era, although Islam was uncommon. Now more than 1 billion people adhere to the main tenets of the faith. Will you?"

Blessed by the question, Rachel focuses on the here and now. "Right now, let's buy *hijab*, sweetheart. You can go to school tomorrow with a new look."

Yerusalem breathes in the statement, "The real me."

Abdul-Tawwab is home in his living room and receives a series of texts from Yerusalem.

Malik, angered, demands to know, "Who is texting you?"

"It's Yerusalem," he shrugs.

"Doesn't she know that's *haram*?" Malik fumes.

"She's a convert, Dad. She doesn't know all the rules," Abdul-Tawwab appeals to his leniency.

"What is she texting you?" Malik's insistence is unbending.

"Pictures of her in *hijab*. She went to the mall to buy scarves. Her mom finally let her wear *hijab*," Abdul announces.

"*Mashallah*. That is great news!" Malik returns to being the supportive father.

Abdul-Tawwab continues texting while watching TV in the sparsely decorated living room. He looks up at his father and reports, "I told her she looks beautiful in *hijab*. Yerusalem said that Noor inspired her."

Malik, nostalgic, walks down memory lane, "Your mother looked beautiful in *hijab*."

Espousing Yerusalem's philosophy that everyone is beautiful, Abdul remarks, "Everyone does."

Malik, who is more down-to-earth, offers, "You're generous. Let's give Yerusalem one of mom's *hijab*. Which scarf?"

Abdul-Tawwab chooses immediately, "The orange one."

Malik, contented, "She'll be so happy. Take it with you to school tomorrow."

Abdul-Tawwab packs the *hijab* with his books.

In the hallway the next day, Jennifer and Yerusalem are putting their books away and taking out what's necessary for soccer. It's time for physical education.

Abdul-Tawwab approaches and delivers Yerusalem his mother's scarf.

"*As-salamu alaikum*, sister. Nice to see you in *hijab*. My father and I want you to have this scarf my mom wore."

"That is so sweet, Abdul-Tawwab," accepting the scarf, Yerusalem exclaims overjoyed, "Please tell Malik I said, 'Thank you!' *Jazakum Allahu Khairan*."

Jennifer feeling left out asks, "Translation, please."

"May Allah reward you with goodness!"

"*Wa iyyaki*," Abdul-Tawwab responds with a wholehearted smile.

"Now I want to study Arabic!" Jennifer exclaims as if seduced by an advertisement.

"Please do. Study with me at the Islamic Institute," Yerusalem invites.

Abdul-Tawwab refocuses the conversation, "Save this discussion for after school. Now it's time to play soccer."

Yerusalem puts the orange scarf in her locker.

Yerusalem feeling elated bubbles up, "And I'll wear your mom's *hijab* on the way home. Thank you again. *Shukran jazeelan.*"

"*Afwan,*" Abdul-Tawwab says not missing a beat.

Jennifer, overeager, translates, "Sounds like a marriage proposal to me."

Yerusalem jokingly asks, "What's a girl to do?" She places her pinky on her lower lip.

Abdul-Tawwab shushes them, "Focus on the game."

Brainy Yerusalem replies, "Soccer, no doubt."

Jennifer and Yerusalem walk ahead of Abdul-Tawwab who restrains his tears. Abdul calls his father.

"Thanks Dad! I gave Yerusalem the *hijab*," Abdul-Tawwab speaks as if no one else can hear.

"Wonderful, son! Why are you tearful?" Malik can hear his son's muffled voice.

"I miss mom."

Malik relates, "We all miss her. She had a pure heart."

Taking a huge step, Abdul-Tawwab requests his father's permission, "Dad, may I ask Yerusalem to marry me? She has mother's heart."

"If you feel that way, let's talk to her parents first and the *sheikh*."

"But dad, I want to know now. I can't wait to talk to her parents and my *imam*. Is it yes or no?" Not a moment passes after Abdul-Tawwab reaches the height of suspense until Yerusalem returns with Jennifer a step behind.

Yerusalem confides, "You're impatient, just like my mother."

Abdul-Tawwab, embarrassed, interrupts the conversation with his father and ends the call. He turns to Yeru. "Yerusalem, you heard all this?"

"Yes," she replies nonchalantly.

Abdul-Tawwab takes the mantle, without the element of surprise. "Will you marry me?"

"Yes, I'll take care of you and doodle our names in my journal. I'll call my mom after the soccer game. She will flip out when she hears this. I'm getting married," Yerusalem says incredulous.

Jennifer who predicted this blurts, "I now pronounce you husband and wife."

"You have no such authority," Yerusalem proclaims.

Jennifer in a mock-menacing voice challenges her best friend, Yerusalem, "See you on the soccer field."

Jennifer runs to the soccer game. The sounds of soccer fill the hallway as the door opens.

"What can I buy you to make this legit?" Abdul-Tawwab asks with a rush of emotion.

"You've already sold me on the idea. To be a part of your family would be an honor," Yerusalem responds wistfully.

"What about your parents? What will your parents say?" Abdul demands to know worriedly.

"My father is a pushover. He accepts my mother's opinion carte blanche," Yerusalem assures him.

Abdul-Tawwab moans, "Less conflict."

Yerusalem is really becoming the peacemaker he expected. She shares her expectations, "Yeah, it's important to keep the peace. Let's get to know each other before we move much further in this direction (She points to her ring finger)."

Abdul-Tawwab's phone plays the *Adhan* for the *Dhuhr* prayer.

Abdul-Tawwab points to the sky as if noticing a minaret, "I think I hear the *Adhan*."

"What better way to consummate a marriage than to enter into a state of *sujood*?" Yerusalem counters.

Yerusalem and Abdul-Tawwab take their prayer rugs out of their lockers and line them up. They pray in the hallway facing Mecca.

After their final *sujood* and an "*As-salamu alaikum wa rahmatullah*" to the right and left, they sit and perform *dhikr*.

As the introduction to what seems like a happy marriage, Abdul-Tawwab turns to his future wife with "I love you, Yerusalem." She wastes no time responding, "I love you, too, habibi."

"Beloved…" Abdul-Tawwab peers deeper and deeper into her soul as they gaze in each other's eyes. They are seated on the floor and they are about to kiss. Then Yerusalem and Abdul-Tawwab roll up their prayer rugs, place them in their respective lockers and race to the soccer field.

"See you on the soccer field!" Yerusalem laughs to herself, thankful they avoided the *haram*.

Abdul-Tawwab competitively hurls the statement, "Boys and girls play on separate teams."

Yerusalem arches her back and lifts up her chin. "May the best team win!"

They run toward the soccer field.

Three years later, Yerusalem holds her son in the local hospital as Abdul-Tawwab wraps his arm around her.

"Let's name him Aylan for the Syrian child who washed upon a Turkish shore," Yerusalem whispers as her baby gurgles. She burps him.

Abdul-Tawwab, a new father, asks, "What does the name 'Aylan' mean?"

"Open field," Yerusalem explains as the light cascades in from the window.

"Like a soccer field, the area I swept clean of leaves," Abdul recalls fondly.

"Yes, for your community service project. I remember you told me you swept both the soccer field and the cemetery."

Abdul-Tawwab, increasing in age, sounds like his father when he lectures, "And remember that the Prophet Muhammad, *Salallahu Alayhi Wasalam*, said when a

Muslim makes *Salat* to please Allah, his sins are shed from him like leaves from a tree."

"Your repentance wipes the slate clean. What a good example," Yerusalem encourages him.

Abdul-Tawwab boldly prays, "I hope our son will be an even better example."

"*In Shaa Allah*," Yerusalem says, bolstered in her faith.

Abdul-Tawwab echoes, "*In Shaa Allah*." After a great pause, Abdul sighs with an expansive heart, "He'll be our Aylan and you'll always be my Yerusalem." Abdul wipes the tightly coiled hair off her face and kisses Yerusalem – first her eyelids, then her collarbone.

"Abdul-Tawwab, you're forever in my soul," Yerusalem says glowingly. She lays the child to sleep in the Virginia hospital bed and coos. "We love you, Aylan."

Words are not enough, but they're a great start.

To honor tradition, Abdul-Tawwab calls the *Adhan* in the right ear of his infant son, Aylan. Aylan wakes from sleep with an adorable smile. This moment is emblazoned in the memory of Yerusalem who has many prayers for her family whom she loves.

Prayers are more than words. Prayer anchors us in our faith. It brings us a sense of peace. Prayers build a home in our hearts for whom and what we most treasure. Those surrounded by the people they love are truly blessed.

Glossary of Names and Terms

Abdul-Tawwab (servant of the Accepter of Repentance) - Popular high school student from a wealthy family

Ahmed (much-praised) - Middle school athlete, Mohammed's sidekick

Dr. Aisha (She who lives; womanly) - Middle school teacher, Ph.D. in education

Dr. Ali (lofty, sublime) – Noor's doctor

Aylan (open field) – infant son of Abdul-Tawwab and Yerusalem. It's a Turkish baby name traditionally for girls

David (beloved) – An elementary school student

Fatima (captivating) - Mature middle school girl

Ibrahim (father of a multitude of nations) - David's father

Jennifer (the fair one) – Yerusalem's friend

Malik (King) – Abdul-Tawwab's father

Mohammed (praiseworthy) - Humble middle school student

Naala (first drink of water) – Nurse

Noor (light) - Malik's wife

Rachel (ewe, one with purity) – Yerusalem's mother

Aunt Saha (enduring) – a friend of Abdul-Tawwab's family

Solomon (peace) – A Jewish high school student

Yerusalem (complete awe or city of peace) – An Ethiopian-American high school student and Muslim convert

Zahara (a flower in bloom) – David's mother

Arabic expressions or Islamic terms

Adhan – Muslim call to prayer

Afwan – You're welcome or sorry

Alaihis salaam - Peace be upon him

Alhamdulillah – Praise be to God

As-salaamu alaikum – Peace be upon you

As-salamu alaikum warahmatulahi wabarakatuh – May the peace, mercy, and blessings of Allah be upon you

Walaikum salaam – And may peace be upon you (appropriate response to As-salamu alaikum)

Da'wah – Call or invitation

Dhikr - Remembrance

Dhuhr – Midday prayer

Dua – Invocation or act of supplication

Hadith – A collection of sayings traditionally narrated by different Islamic sources with varying levels of authenticity

Haram – Unlawful, forbidden

Hijab – Veil, head covering

Isa – Jesus

Jahaliyyah – The period of ignorance before the revelation of the Qur'an

Jazakum Allahu Khairan – May Allah reward you with goodness

Wa iyyaki – And goodness to you also

Sheikh – A leader in a Muslim community or organization

Imam – A person who leads prayer in a mosque

Inna lillahi wa inna ilayhi raji'un – We surely belong to Allah and to Him we shall return

In Shaa Allah – God-willing

Janazah – Islamic funeral prayer

Jannah - Paradise

Maghrib – Evening prayer

Mash'Allah- God has willed it

Ruqiyah – Spiritual healing or Islamic exorcism

SalAllahu alayhi wasalam – May the peace and blessings of Allah be upon him

Shukran jazeelan – Thank you very much

Subhanahu Wa Ta'ala – The most glorified, the most high

Subhanallah – Glory to God

Sujood – An act of prostration

Sunnah – Daily life and recorded practice of the Prophet Muhammad, peace and blessings be upon him, and his Companions

Tahajjud – Non-obligatory prayers after midnight and before Fajr

Wudu – Ritual ablutions before prayer

39836111R00054

Made in the USA
Middletown, DE
26 January 2017